D0465072

Donated by the

**WILRUSS CHILDREN'S
LIBRARY TRUST**

CONTRA COSTA COUNTY LIBRARY

Copyright © 1994 by Nick Sharratt
All rights reserved.

First U.S. paperback edition 1996

The Library of Congress has cataloged the hardcover edition as follows:

Sharratt, Nick.
Mrs. Pirate / Nick Sharratt. — 1st U.S. ed.
Summary: Mrs. Pirate goes shopping, alternating
her purchases between household items and nautical gear.
ISBN 1-56402-249-8 (hardcover)
[1. Pirates — Fiction.   2. Shopping — Fiction.   3. Stories in rhyme.]   I. Title.
PZ8.3.S5323Mr   1994
[E] — dc20   93-878

ISBN 1-56402-684-1 (paperback)

2 4 6 8 10 9 7 5 3 1

Printed in Hong Kong

This book was typeset in Helvetica Educational.
The pictures were done in watercolor and ink.

Candlewick Press
2067 Massachusetts Avenue
Cambridge, Massachusetts 02140

Mrs. Pirate

Nick Sharratt

CANDLEWICK PRESS

CAMBRIDGE, MASSACHUSETTS

When Mrs. Pirate
went shopping,
she bought
an apple pie

and a patch
for her eye,

a bar of soap

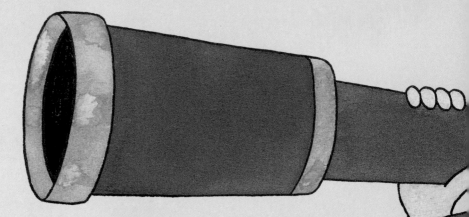

and a telescope,

an onion
and a carrot

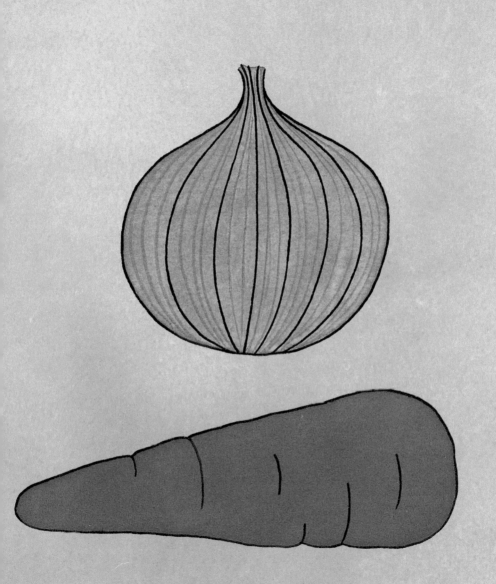

and a red-
and-green
parrot,

underwear made
to measure,

and a chest full
of treasure,

buttons for
her coat

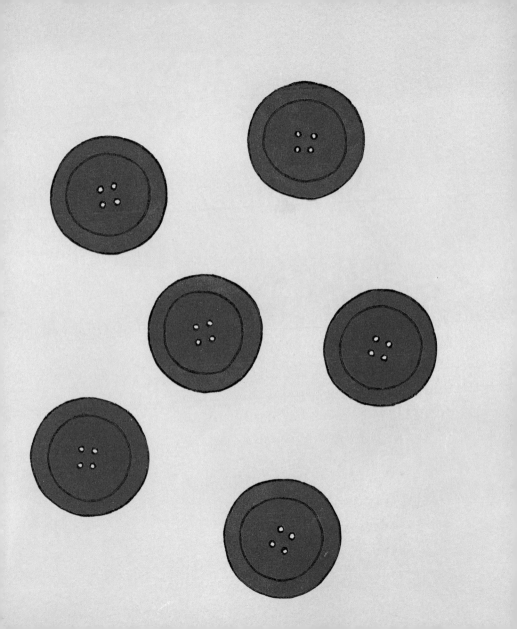

and a big
sailing boat,

a box full
of tea,

and some sea.